UNDERSEA ADVENTURES OF OLLI AND FRIENDS

Renate Schalk Schreiner

AuthorHouse™
1663 Liberty Drive
Bloomington, IN 47403
www.authorhouse.com
Phone: 1 (800) 839-8640

Because of the dynamic nature of the Internet, any web addresses or links contained in this book may have changed since publication and may no longer be valid. The views expressed in this work are solely those of the author and do not necessarily reflect the views of the publisher, and the publisher hereby disclaims any responsibility for them.

This book is printed on acid-free paper.

ISBN: 978-1-7283-2347-3 (sc)
ISBN: 978-1-7283-2346-6 (e)
ISBN: 978-1-7283-2348-0 (hc)

Library of Congress Control Number: 2019912201

Print information available on the last page.

Published by AuthorHouse 08/21/2019

"Good friends". There is a deeper meaning to it than just two words which forms a thread which connects all of us. Race, color of skin, choice of attire and more does not matter to friends.

Renate has successfully shown just such a thread in the undersea animal world and thus inspired me to create the illustrations for it.

These friendships can set a good example above water as well. They can show children the way it can work. As a former teacher Renate was able to observe this first hand. In this book she shows experience and emotions.

For these delightful writings she will continue to count on my artistic help.

— **Udo Raumschuessel**

From Renate Schalk Schreiner's first dream of Olli the octopus, she knew she was on a path toward bringing her underwater creatures to vibrant life. Olli whispered stories to her bright imagination and she swam along with him. "Undersea Adventures of Olli and Friends" is sure to be a classic for children and adults to enjoy, wrapped in the multi-tentacle hug of Renate's lead octopus character.

Long live life in the deep waters of our earth! Long live Olli!

— Antonia Allegra

ACKNOWLEDGEMENTS

I would like to dedicate this book to my good friend, Michele Mills, who inspired me to write these stories. Without her it would not have happened.

I would also like to thank my good friend and mentor, Antonia Allegra, whose encouragement and belief in me kept me going.

To my cousin, Udo Raumschuessel, goes my unending gratitude for designing and drawing the illustrations for these stories. His artistic talents made them come alive.

My late mother, Melitta Richter, was the one with the poetry talents. I am glad she passed them on to me. Danke Mutti.

CONTENTS

THE TRICKY BIRTHDAY PRESENT

Olli, the young octopus, is frolicking in the sea.
Today is his birthday; he's as happy as can be.
Someone handed him a basket full of toys,
Now he's trying them to see which he most enjoys.
A rubber ducky, not so much; a football, not for me.

Now, wait a minute, down below is something I must see.
He brings it up to take a look and cannot figure out
That little thing bright red and round, he stares at with a pout.
Looking closer now he sees a name that spells yo-yo.
What in Neptune's name is that and what will make it go?

The instructions now he grabs and studies carefully,
That looks easy, I can see, as easy as can be.
He starts with one and next another, there are eight of them, you see.
Oh! What fun to play with them on the bottom of the sea.
Here he goes with 1, 2, 3, then more of them, yippee!
Now all eight of them are up like letting birds go free.

Cat in the cradle, the boomerang and more,
Each arm does something different that is quite a chore.
His eyes, they follow each little toy,
Go back and forth with lots of joy.
Until they cross, his head does hurt and trouble comes galore.
The fun is gone; he does not want to play this anymore.

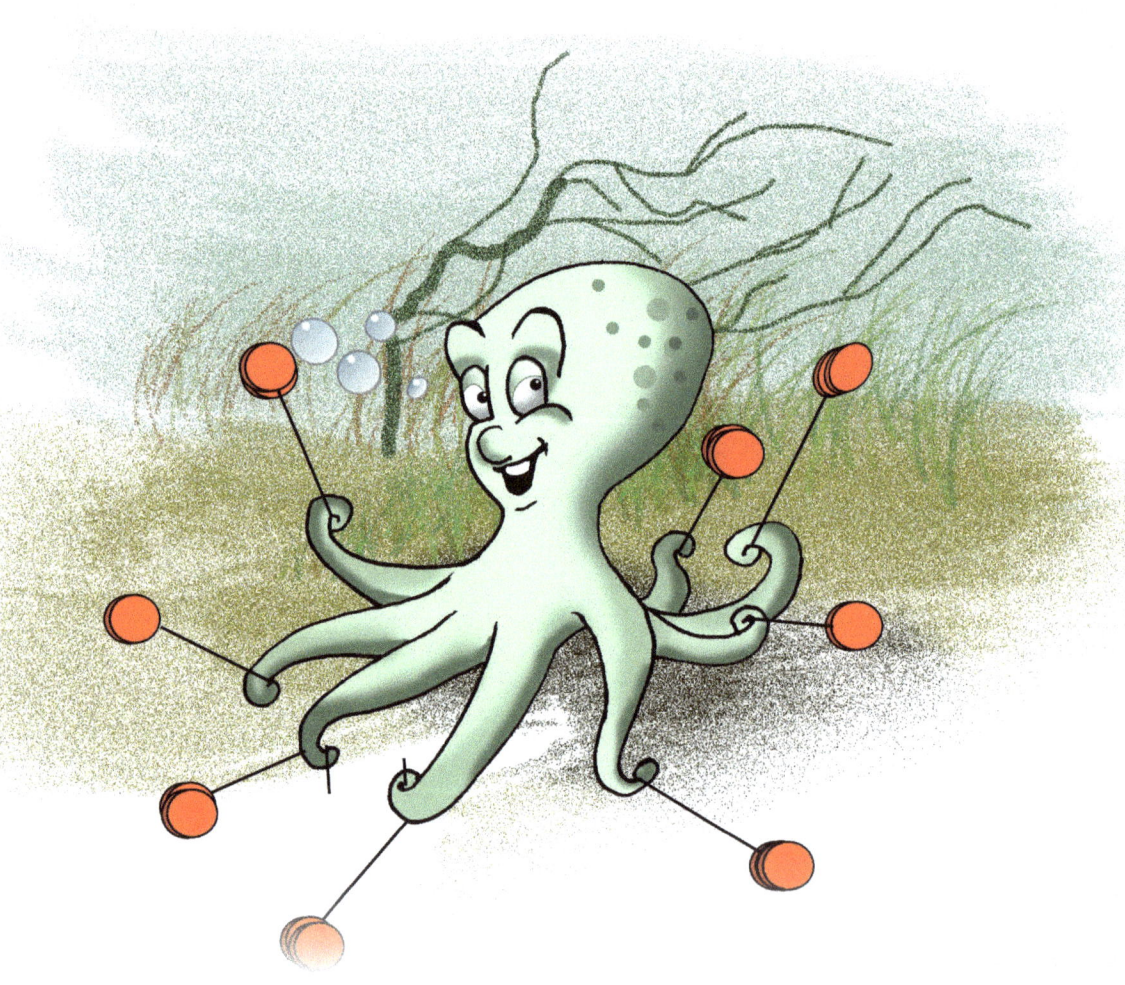

The strings, they tangle one by one, flying all around.
Until poor Olli, struck with fear is all wrapped up and bound.
"Oh me! Oh my! What will I do with tentacles like these?"
"Come over here, my ocean friends, will someone help me, PLEASE?"

Along comes a clown fish with his friends, swimming near the ground;
"Hush now and listen. What's making that great sound?"
They see poor Olli and they laugh at this unusual sight,
But Olli cannot laugh at all. He is stricken with sheer fright.

"Come help me please, untie the strings, they're given me a gash."
The laughter stops and 1, 2, 3; they're with him in a dash.
Over and under, through and around,
Each clownfish is busy, to get him unbound.

In no time at all Olli is free,
He stretches his tentacles with a much relieved "Whee."
"Get ready for a group hug from a thankful...me."

Eight yo-yo's are on the ocean floor,
Eight little clownfish those now adore.
Off they go with their gifts so rare,
I sure wish I could have been there.

OLLI GOES TO SCHOOL

It's a beautiful morning at the bottom of the sea.
Young Olli swims along, so happy and carefree.
"Good morning, Miss Anemone, how are you today?
Won't you cut loose and come with me so we can laugh and play?"

"Oh, no, dear Olli that won't do. I'm stuck here in the sand
And must remain where I grew up. I hope you understand."

"Good bye, I'll have to leave you with your friends,
To sway with the breeze on which your life depends."

So off he goes until he hears a swooshing sound nearby.
It's something that he'd never heard. It almost makes him cry.
Now, what is this? What can it be?
I must go close enough to see.

A school of fish is swimming by, not watching where they go.
Poor Olli gets amongst them but can't get with the flow.
They spin him all around, that leaves him quite perplexed,
Wondering in his dizziness what may be coming next.

The little guppies realize their uncontrolled behavior.
They turn around and go right back to be poor Ollie's savior.

"Excuse us please, dear octopus, we are in a hurry.
School starts soon and we don't want the teacher to worry."

"School you say, did I hear right? You want to make me sad?
What do you do there? How's it done? Is it something bad?"

"Oh no, it is a lot of fun, we love to go to school,
We learn new things each day and think it's absolutely cool.
We play neat games, do sports and more,
All things we never did before."

Olli now is curious and wants to know much more
About this school and learning things, on the ocean floor.

"Why don't you come along with us and check it out," they say,
"And meet the teacher, wonderful, the mermaid Leelofay.
We're sure she won't object at all to someone like you,
That brings this Kindergarten class to twelve, woohoo."

Off they go, Olli in their middle,
He's so proud and fit as a fiddle.
They reach the lagoon and it's quite late,
Just before Miss Leelofay closes the gate.

She invites little Olli to sit next to her,
If he was a cat, he would now start to purr.
"I am going to school; I can learn and have friends.
What a beautiful day, I wish it never ends."

As the day progresses and the lessons are learned,
They all get star stickers, proudly earned.
Olli is glad that he came along,
He adores Miss Leelofay, that can't be wrong.
Aware of the guppie's claim about school,
He also now thinks that it's absolutely cool.

THE GREAT SCARE

School is out and Olli and friends
are swimming along holding "hands".
They are laughing and joking having much fun
Enjoying the day in the shimmering sun.

Suddenly Olli has such a strange feeling,
Something that is not at all appealing.
He senses that someone follows behind,
That does not appear the friendly kind.

Olli turns to see what it may be
And stares into a face that's horrid to see.
A shark is there looking for his lunch.
Olli doesn't know that yet but clearly has a hunch.

He stretches out his tentacles and reaches for his peers.
"Stay close to me, real close, I say", for he can sense their fears.
All in a huddle, their fins are frozen,
Something they would never have chosen
Unless they were playing a game of tag;
But now realize that it's not a gag.
All 12 are stricken with so much fright,
Wishing they would be way out of sight.
The shark moves closer sporting a grin
Showing two rows of sharp teeth within.

Then suddenly the whole scene turns dark,
Nothing to be seen, not even the shark.

What happened? They sure cannot figure it out,
Then the monster withdraws with an angry shout:
"I'll get you next time when I can see where you are!"
They all hear his voice now from afar.

Still clinging together in Olli's embrace
They slowly can see each other's face.
"What happened just now and what kept us alive?
We all were sure we would not survive."

They are looking at Olli, who is black as ink,
so scared that he can hardly blink.
From where did this cloud of blackness appear?
Nothing like that was anywhere near.
They check out each other and Olli as well,
Until they hear their new friend yell:

"That black cloud, it came out of me!
Now that is something I never did see.
It must be a fluid I can push out like a cape,
For my protection, so I can escape.
How glad I am we were together today,
Now we are safe and can swim away.

THE CELEBRATION

The Fiesta Lagoon, by the moon full and round,
Is the place King Neptune looked for, and found
For a celebration with all the trimmings,
He now best starts with dreams of beginnings.

Princess Leelofay, his oldest, will turn 17 that day
And the Monarch wants to have a great display
Of sparkly decorations, fun games and much more,
Talent shows, plus cake not seen before.

Spectacular fireworks at the end of the night
To light up the ocean for each guest's delight.
He invites all the students from Leelofay's school,
He knows she'll enjoy that, for he is no fool.

As the evening arrives, sea folks stream in,
Now is the time for the show to begin.
King Neptune's large family, himself on his throne,
All royal and mighty with a crown of rare stone.
Miss Leelofay looks like a princess today,
Though rarely displays herself this way.
She is a free spirit; she knows her own mind,
She's strong-willed at times, but ever so kind.

The life at the castle was not hers to bear,
She left all her brothers and sisters back there.
The work of a teacher was her heart's desire,
From that job she will not soon retire.

But tonight she's a princess with a birthday as well,
"What's going on, Papa? Please make it clear as a bell."

"In honor of your special night
I invited your guests to this undersea site.
It's your favorite of all, here in the lagoon,
Especially enchanted by the full moon."

He raises his trident, now red-hot with fire,
For this evening he has but one desire
That all who are here and all who are small
Will not be disturbed by the creatures so tall.
Creating a force-shield around them now,
He's king, and knows how to do it somehow.
Zap goes the trident, with sizzle and spark,
Now they are safe in this magic park.

The first performance goes to Olli and the guppies.
They are excited as new little puppies.
They sing a song, their first one ever,
They composed it themselves and it's rather clever.
The princess has glistening tears in her eyes,
But behind the fan shows not that she cries.

King Neptune is pleased with a wink and applause,
Olli and friends are proud when they pause.
They bow to the king and their little hearts pound,
With smiles on their faces they're turning around
To swim back to their seats, for the show goes on.
To do that, the band leader lifts his baton.
The trumpet fish trumpet, the blow fish blow
While sea grass does a dance below.
The full moon illumines with its wonderful light,
It turns out to be a spectacular night.

The star fish turn cartwheels, the clown fish are funny,
Sea horses swim races, for the show, not sea money.
A bubble blowing contest is on the agenda now,
Who has the biggest one? It's Olli! WOW!

The night gets late but they do not care,
There is more to come, they want to share.
No school tomorrow, they all can sleep long...
Now listen, I hear the birthday song.

Olli stops fidgeting and they join in,
Standing much closer, fin-next-to-fin.
The princess declares it is time for the treat,
A huge cake is brought in for all folks to eat.
Made of cucumbers, kelp, seaweed and more,
All the tastes that sea creatures adore.
When they had their fill and settle back down,
In comes a puffer fish dressed like a clown.

"We all had a good time here in the lagoon,
But now it must end as the sun chases the moon.
Before we depart I invite all of you,
To thank King Neptune, it's the right thing to do
For his kindness and generosity,
That allowed all of us under the sea,
To be part of this special festivity.
Now join me to give him a finny big hand,
Great enough to stir up the sand.

To bring the celebration to a conclusion
Sit back and marvel at the illusion
Of fireworks high over the lagoon,
And the gates to go home will open soon."

MOVING DAY

Olli wakes up not feeling quite right.
Again he had a horrible night.
His arms are crooked and his head has a sore,
He hurts all over, right down to the core.

My sleeping arrangement somehow feels tight,
Something here is not at all right.
What could have happened and what made it so?
I have no answers...off to school I go.

Miss Leelofay surely can help out,
She always knows what it's about.

"Olli, dear Olli, what happened to you?
The look on you is oh so new."

He tells his friends and the teacher, too,
Of the terrible night, he has just been through.

"This way of sleeping is not much fun.
I do not know what can be done."

Miss Leelofay smiles and explains to the class,
The terrible cramped feeling will certainly pass.

"You are growing in size, my dear little one,
It happens to all of us when we are young."

"I don't want to do this," is his reply,
"I can't understand this growing-up-and why?"

"Everything grows and so do you,
There is nothing at all that you can do
To stop it from happening so wait a while
It all will work out in just the right style.
She continues:

You feel tight when you sleep at night?
Perhaps the size of your bed is not right.
Maybe the rock you use when you rest
Needs to be bigger or stronger, at best
Why don't your friends all help you out?"

"What an adventure," they all shout,
As it is moving day for Olli, their friend,
And they are happy to lend him a "hand."

Olli is thinking about it all
Then stands up, straight and tall:
"I'll do it, right after school is done,
This adventure should be fun."

So the group takes off, thrilled as can be.
"We'll find you a new home just wait and see."

While searching and scouting and looking all over,
There is something new they discover
On the bottom of the undisturbed sea.
They are gazing and wondering-what it could be.

Small mounds of colors are strewn around there,
Like dumped garbage left without care.
Something is moving all around,
Right below them on the ocean ground.

Olli now grabs it and sees legs sticking out,
"Come out, whomever," he says with a shout!
At once they see a tiny head lurk,
"I'm Hermi, the crab," he says, with a smirk.

"I'm Olli and friends, may we ask you, please,
What you are doing among the looks of these?"

"This shell that I'm in is getting too tight,
I must find a new one for the night.
That's why I'm here to pick one now,
Snails grow bigger shells' when needed, somehow."

"I'm doing the same Hermi the crab,
My present quarters are tight and drab.
I like the colors you found today.
It was nice to have met you, now we are on our way."

"Olli, here's the perfect place for you,
It's cheerful, bright, and, brand new;
It's a coral reef filled with crevices galore."

"I'll try it out and look no more."

He slinks into a hole and feels this is it,
But his friends are now having a fit.

"Olli, this place is red, but you are not
A hungry predator will find this spot."

"Don't worry, I know a trick, you see,
I can change color wherever I'll be."

The group is happy that Olli found his niche,
An amazing thing is happening without a hitch.

"Goodbye to you all, I'll stay here and sleep.
Thanks for your help, this place I will keep."

SEA-HORSING AROUND

School is out for the summer, hurray!
Olli is delighted and expects each day
To have an adventure, or maybe two,
What that could be, he has to think through.

He loves his teacher, don't get me wrong,
And the friendship with the guppies is quite strong.
Alone he wants to be for awhile,
To figure out if that is his style.

I can catch up with my friends later on,
To find out from all what they have done
To make their vacation as nice as can be,
For now I just have to wait and see.

Swimming along without a care,
He enters scenery to him quite rare.
The water is shallow and eelgrasses grow,
Many, so many, all in a row.

Something else now catches his eye,
It is a brood of very small fry.
He's never seen them so near before
And now ventures closer to explore.
He almost collides with a seahorse there,
If he were to leave now that wouldn't be fair.

"Excuse me. I'm Olli and who are you?"

"I'm Charlie, the seahorse, how do you do?
I'm out here with my little brood,
All eight of them in a playful mood.
They go all over everywhere without care
And wear me out, that gives me a scare.
I can't count if all of them are still here,
If they are then there is nothing to fear.

He continues...
Life was much easier before they hatched,
In a pouch on my body they were attached.
I knew exactly where they were
But since they hatched I would prefer
To have more control, I need some assistance.

"I'll help", said Olli without resistance.
"What if I entertain your small fry?
To give you a rest, now don't be shy."

"Come here little sea monsters, hear my plan.
I'll be a carousel, pay attention if you can.
Each one of you holds on to one arm,
Wrap your tails around it, works like a charm.
Here we go now, yippee and hurray!
This is the way to have fun and play."

Faster and faster he spins around,
The little seahorses don't make a sound.
When he goes higher and falls down quick,
He is hoping that none of them will get sick.

Now they are squealing with delight,
Clinging to Olli ever so tight.
Slowly he brings them down to the ground,
"Up again, please," they cry with one sound.

"Alright then, if you think you can last,
This time I will go really fast."

He moves his arms like waving goodbye,
This time he does not hear them cry
Faster, go faster... "Now you can stop,
We are done for today." They let go and flop
Into the eelgrass, all tuckered out.
Charlie, their dad, has a smile on his snout.

"Olli that was kind of you
Now that they're tired I can rest too.
Thank you so much for coming by,
Don't be a stranger, show up and say 'Hi'."

SILLY DAY

Oh, what a boring day is this,
I must confess that I do miss
My friends to share adventures galore,
This going alone I don't want anymore.

Olli sets out to find his buddies now
They have been looking for him anyhow.
"Olli, the oldest, you have to say
What we could do that is crazy today."

"Put on the thinking caps, we are smart,
The more we think, the sooner we start.
I've got it! I've got it! Let's be silly today,
And have a dress-up party, I say."

"A dress-up party, what do you mean?
Something like that we've never seen."

"Exactly, that's why we should try it out,
Come on now, please. Don't anyone pout.
We'll look all over the ocean floor
For stuff to dress up with and then look some more
For colorful grasses, shells and such.
Things we admire and can touch.
Now go, but let us meet again soon,
Let's say we assemble here at noon."

Olli is off to the shell dumping place,
Finds eight of them with a smile on his face.
One for each arm, what fun that will be,
Now for a hat, he soon finds three!

Back I must go to see what they found
Lying right there on the ocean ground.
Maybe they picked up seaweed and kelp,
And need some advice or possibly help
To decide what works best for each one,
Oh, won't that be silly and great fun?

They gather again at noon, as was said,
Showing their treasures in blue, green and red.
"Alright now everyone, dress up yourselves
With grasses and seaweeds, looking like "elves".
When ready we will have a silly parade,
Let's hurry so the daylight won't fade."

As they get dressed they giggle and holler,
Some of the guppies now look taller.
Olli has placed the shells he has found
On all of his arms, safe and sound.
He's walking the floor like he's on high heels,
To learn how to do it and how it feels.

One hat, now garnished with eelgrass and coral,
Gives it a look that's rather floral.
"Are you ready, my friends, can we start our march?
From here we will go to the great coral arch.
Something is missing to liven the show.
Let's call a trumpet fish so he can blow
The rhythm we are marching to
I'll start a song, join in, please do."

As they are making their way to the arch,
Other animals are joining the march.
They're clapping and singing and shouting "Hurray!
What an outstanding silly day."

By now a crowd has gathered around,
"What an idea the children have found
To entertain themselves and us,
They certainly deserve an A+."

At the end of the day they all feel so great,
They are happy and silly and tired. It's late.

AGATHA TURTLE

On another day of Olli's vacation,
He ventures out, changing location
To see how fast he can swim and dive,
He makes it up to hour five.

Now he is tired, so tired in fact,
That he is afraid he may be attacked
And would not be able to get away.
"I think it is better when I stay
Around here and recover awhile,
In fact I'll do it right here on this pile".
He lowers himself onto a beautiful rock,
Of the intricate pattern he's now taking stock.
As he admires his resting place,
The "rock" starts to move at a slow pace.

A startled Olli is now awake,
What's going on, for blue water's sake?
When he looks closer his head starts to spin,
There's a head, and legs, and tail, but no fin.
This is too strange; I have to find out,
What this place is all about.

"Who are you? What are you, tell me, please do,
To me you are so incredibly new.
Are you a fish? But no fins do I see."

"Fins are of no use to me.
I'm a turtle, I swim, but need legs even more,
When it is time to go ashore."

"A turtle you say, is that what you are?
You must have come from another star.
I never saw anyone looking like you.
My name is Olli, how do you do?
I'm an octopus; I'm still rather small,
In a few years I will be quite tall."

"Agatha Turtle is my name
And I am doing just the same.
I used to be small starting out,
But growing, that's what it's all about.
I've been around for many a year,
With my protection there's not much to fear.
My head, legs and tail tuck in, what a blessing,
To protect my soft belly the ground I'm addressing."

"That is so awesome and will keep you secure,
You don't fit into a small cave, for sure
To hide 'til the danger has gone away
And unfold your body again this way.
That's why you look so calm swimming here,
To enjoy your life without great fear.
Agatha, I'd like to ask you much more,
While we are here on the ocean floor."

"Stay on my back and I will give you a ride
And show you how the ocean is wide.
What is your question, Olli? Speak now.
Hang on so you won't fall off somehow."

"Agatha, do you have children, pray tell?
Are they grown up, are they well?"

"Many babies I have had in my time,
Probably now up to one hundred and nine.
Could be much more, I can't count too well,
That's all the numbers I can tell.
When I am ready to lay my eggs,
I swim to the surface then need my legs
To go to the beach where I dig a ditch
And lay many eggs without a hitch.
Covered with wet sand they will not dry out,
The sun warms them, that's what it's about.

Agatha continues...
Buried, they stay there for awhile
'Till they are ready to hatch from that pile.
They dig themselves out of their hiding place
And run to the sea at a hurried pace.
They need to get to the water fast,
Failing to do that they will not last.
Once they reach the ocean side,
They can swim out with the tide."

"Do you ever see your children again?
How would you even know them then?"

"Maybe one day we will meet,
If they remember me, that would be sweet.
That is the way life works down here,
I hope I made myself quite clear."

"What a wonderful story you have told,
I will never forget it no matter how old
I become and share with my peers,
I bet they also will be all ears.
It was nice to have met you, Agatha, dear,
But now it is time to get out of here."

THE FIELD TRIP

Vacations are over and all have returned
To the school where all year they have learned
Many new things they had never known,
Now that knowledge is their own.

"While school was out you had fun, so did I.
Today we'll do something new, that's why
I need your attention, all eyes on me, please,
To learn the instructions I give you with ease.

You all did good work and are ready for this,
An outing away, it's called the Abyss.
We call it a field trip and learn right out there,
Pretending the classroom is anywhere.
There is something exciting I want you to see
Make sure you stay close and follow me."

Their eyes light up like never before,
They wonder what Miss Leelofay has in store
For them and what it could be
That on their outing they will see.

"What is it? Where is it? Please let us know,"
Olli asks, "before we go,"

"Oh no, my dear little ones just wait awhile
'Till we get there, now please go single file."

The excitement grows as they swim out together,
What a blessing to have such good weather.
The sea is calm, the sun shines bright,
Soon they are at the promised site.

Everyone now is as stunned as can be,
Something like that they never did see.
Their questions are heard everywhere,

"What is it and how did it get there?"

Before them, they see a ship that went down
A long time ago, all withered and brown.

"A ship? Who used it?" They now ask quick.

"Nobody now, that's why it looks sick.
At one time though, a long time ago,
It rode on the water above us, quite so.
Humans were on it, they built it like this
As you now see it in the Abyss."

Their excitement is building their questions come fat,

"What are humans, and why didn't they last?"

"Humans are people who live on the land,
Above us, you must understand.
A different species they surely are,
Without air down here they won't get far.
They swim, they dive and have fun as we do
In the water but when they are through,
Whey must return to the earth above.
Boating is something most all of them love

She continues...

This ship was used to travel the ocean.
They did that quite often with great devotion.
Now go, be explorers and see what you find,
Keep what you learn all in your mind.
I'll call you again when it's time to go back,
Waiting here with your favorite snack."

Off they go in all directions
To examine the shipwreck in all its sections.
In and out over and yonder,
They're everywhere and look with great wonder
At the ship and how it was made.
What became of the humans? Why did they fade?

"Miss Leelofay, please come take a look,
At the front of the ship, there is a big hook.
What's above, it is to us so new,
We all think it looks just like you.
That figure there is missing a tail,
Something was added that looks quite frail"

"Those are legs that humans need.
Good observers you are, indeed.
I could not walk with my tail or stand
On the earth, like they do so grand."

"Have you ever seen humans Miss Leelofay?"

"From afar only that's all I can say,
About my knowledge of humans today.
It's getting late, let's leave the Abyss.
Go home and really think about this
Lesson you learned so well today,
It will come in handy one day, I daresay."

TOOTIE

RED BALLOONS

Olli and the guppies are out and about.
As usual they are happy, they laugh and shout.
They are looking for an adventure on such a nice day,
Not watching where they are going, they lose their way.

"Where are we? At this place we've never been,
Alone or even with our kin.
Hush now, quiet, calm down and you hear,
Wonderful sounds from somewhere near."

The higher they rise, the louder it is,
They've never heard anything like this.
It sounds like music, for red star sake,
But different from what they usually make.

Above them is something that darkens the sea,
They swim around it so they can see.
What a surprise, it looks like a ship,
But different than the one from the field trip.

That one was withered, old and rusty,
This one looks shiny and not even dusty.
Heads above water to see better yet,
There is nothing to fear; now they're all set.

As all seems in order they now can enjoy
The scene on the ship that looks like a toy.
Their eyes get wide, as wide as can be,
They can hardly believe what they now see.
The ship is decorated with balloons, all red,
To see even better they go further ahead.

"Look at those bubbles tied up in a row,
That is making quite a show.
It must be someone's favorite color."
All of a sudden they start to holler.
"HUMANS! They are on the ship we see.
Tall ones and shorter, I now see three."

The little one there is having a ball,
Dancing around the other's so tall.
Her hair is the color of Miss Leelofay,
The red dress and crown give it away.
She is having a birthday, turning seven today.
A bright red ribbon adorns her hair,
She is sweet and happy and quite fair.
Because she loves the ocean so much
The family gave it that special touch
To celebrate on the open sea,
No wonder she's happy as can be.

"Olli, you already read so well–
Can you make out what the writing does spell
That's on the front of the ship in big print?
Go closer so you don't have to squint."

Olli is proud to be asked by his mates,
He reads the words and then relates:
"The name on the ship I see is TOOTIE,
I bet that's the name of the little cutie
That is having the party, how special that is,
She'll never forget a day like this."

When Olli read the name to his friends out loud,
The little girl at the railing appears, so proud
As if she has heard him calling her name,
And now is glad that closer she came.
She has a big smile and an extremely keen eye,
With that she does the friends below spy.

"Hello, down there, I love you all."

Their little hearts pound like a bouncing ball.
She loves us, the sweet thing above so high,
For a minute they all act rather shy,
Then they shout out, "We love you too!
Enjoy your birthday until it is through."

Tootie unties her curly blond hair
And throws the ribbon into the air.
It lands directly at Olli's location,
He takes it as an invitation
To pick it up and take along
For Miss Leelofay, that doesn't seem wrong.

"Goodbye little Tootie we must go,
It was great to have met you, we enjoyed it so."
The friends take the ribbon and hold on tight,
Not to get lost for it is nearly night.

At school the next morning they have much to say
To their teacher about the human birthday.
They present her the ribbon, how proud they are
To have brought it to her from afar.

She ties up her hair with a big bow,
They all are in awe, for they love her so.

ELUSA MEDUSA

It has been a glorious, busy day.
Olli is tired and on his way
To the coral reef, where he sleeps at night.
A little snooze would feel just right.

He settles down in his comfortable space
When something is shining across his face.
He opens his eyes and is now wide awake,
What could that have been, maybe a mistake?

There it goes again, another light flashes.
By now he is up, from his bed he dashes
To see what is above him now,
And spots the most wonderful creatures. WOW!

Their beauty and movements to him are so strange,
Looking like bells, they must live out of range.
I must know who they are and where they go now,
This is too intriguing to miss anyhow.

He forgets his nap and ventures out
To inquire what this is all about.

Most of the strangers have floated past,
One of the small ones is following last.

"Hello, little stranger, may I know your name?
Where are you going, are you playing a game?
I am an octopus, Olli's my name,
I'd like to find out if you're someone of fame."

The little creature stops in mid-swim
And turns to Olli to look at him.
"So you're an octopus. I've heard that before,
You are the kind that lives close to shore.
I'm Elusa Medusa of the jelly fish kind,
I'm not really a fish as you clearly will find."

"Elusa Medusa, what a beautiful name,
Please tell me more from whence you came
And where are you going, so many of you?
Do you think it's alright if I go too?"

"We would be delighted if you joined us tonight,
You will have the pleasure to see quite a sight.
We're on the way to the blue lagoon
To perform a dance there by the full moon.
I am still too young to be part of the show,
But wish in my heart it would not be so.
I'll sit with you and answer your questions,
Unless you have any other suggestions."

"It will be my pleasure to go with you,
Just tell me what I should say or do."

Together they follow the jelly fish swarm
To the lagoon where the water is warm.
There they witness the most stunning dance
Of gentle movements just right for romance.

So many colors they now see
Some even glow, how can that be?
That's what was shining on my face today
When for a nap in my bed I lay.
I'm glad I woke up while I was still in it,
I wouldn't have missed this, not even a minute.
They are sitting in wonder and awe of it all,
When both of them hear a distant voice call:

"Come join us and do just as we do,
Stay here until the night is through."

And so their dances in moonlight begin.-
"Be careful, dear Olli. Do not come too near.
I may accidentally touch you, I fear.
My tentacles are a part of me
For my protection and feeding, you see.
They can harm you when we touch.
I don't want to do that. I like you too much.

She goes on...
When humans do come in contact with us,
They always put up such a terrible fuss
Because our tentacles give a mighty sting,
To humans that is not a small thing."

With respectful distance they continue the dance,
Not giving the stinging or hurting a chance.
They are pulsating, propelling, gyrating as well
Having a great time as one can tell.
Most jelly fish tentacles are long and pale,
They follow behind like a pretty bride's veil.
Their bodies are translucent for the most part,
They truly resemble great works of art.
Caught up in the activity are Elusa and Olli,
Having a splendid time being so jolly.

Time slips away as time can do.
They now realize that the night is through.
The dance has ended, all jellies are leaving,
It's time for Olli and his retrieving.

"Good bye, Elusa, my dear new friend,
I wish this night did not have to end.
I hope we will see each other once more,
Dancing with you is what I adore."

"I loved to dance with you as well,
Perhaps we'll do this again, who can tell."

STARLET STARFISH...AND RAYMIE TOO

Unbeknownst to Olli, new neighbors moved in one night.
When he got up next morning, he witnessed quite a site.
Five sea stars, known as starfish, were moving all around,
Looking for their breakfast, before him on the ground.

He'd never seen the likes of them, but heard that they exist,
Here was his chance to meet them now, one not to be missed.
How can they run or even walk, with no legs anywhere,
It looked quite funny, but to laugh, he didn't think was fair.
His curiosity was strong; it would not let him rest
Until he'd meet the newcomers, he thought that would be best.

Gliding over to a starfish that was near to him,
He takes an even closer look and then asks, on a whim:
"Good morning, new neighbors, who may you, be?
I've watched you closely. It's unclear to me
How can you move and be so swift
When I don't see legs, if you catch my drift?
I am an octopus and Olli is my name.
I introduced myself to you, be kind and do the same."

"Gladly I will tell you who your new neighbors are,
You may already know that I'm a sea star.
My name is Starlet Starfish, I am known for that
Come and meet my friends right off the bat.
I'm so glad to meet you, fellow neighbor Olli,
It seems to me you could be witty, curious and jolly."

"You are right on all accounts; I'm looking for new thrills,
Are you up for some excitement, the kind that gives you chills?"
Before I say what is on my mind
Introduce your friends, if you'd be so kind?"

One call brings them over to where they are standing,
Starlet introduces them, as they are landing.
"Olli meet Crusty, Spiny, Red and Racer,
He among us is the outstanding pacer.
The rest of us try to keep up with him,
Sometimes our chances are really slim."

"It sure was nice to meet all of you here,
But I'm still not clear how you do it, I fear.
I know you move fast, I've seen that just now.
You sure must have legs, to do it somehow."

"Oh, yes, we have legs called tube feet, in fact,
When hunting for food they make quite an impact.
If you lift me right up, you will find,
All five of us have the very same kind."

As Olli turns Starlet around to find out,
The others lift arms to show there's no doubt.

"Now that you know what makes us go,
What's on your mind that excites you so?"

"How would you like to run a race?
Everyone at your own pace?
I'll referee and give you the sign,
Please be good sports and do not decline.
That's what I dreamed up in my mind,
Do indulge me, if you don't mind."

"Yes, oh yes, that sounds like much fun,
Line up so Olli can call the run."

"On your marks, get ready go, go, go,
Use all your tube feet, do not be slow."

They are running to the coral bridge and back,
Olli is cheering so loud he may crack.
Five sea stars are running as fast as they can,
Our friend is amazed and now a big fan.
They gather to say they enjoyed the run,
"Want to add more excitement and fun?"

A velvety stingray, all flat and grey
Lowers himself to their level to stay.

"How much more pleasure can you offer us, say,
And who might you be we are meeting today?"

"I beg your pardon, how rude of me,
I am Raymie, the stingray, as you can see.

"Say, Raymie, what could you offer us now,
That would give this fun day a really great WOW?"

"Oh, I could take you on my back for a ride,
And show you how through the ocean I glide.
Won't you hop on and I'll "fly" like a bird,
Looking at me it may sound absurd.
It works for me and I do rather well,
What do you say; will you go for a spell?"

"Absolutely," is the happy reply,
"Now let's figure out how to comply.
I have a thought and it might just work,
If you follow instructions and do not jerk.
All five of you starfish climb up on my top,
Attach yourselves so you will not flop.
Watch out for my eyes for I want to see,
Where we are going, so leave them free."

They do as Olli said and squeal in delight,
Presenting themselves a humorous sight.
Raymie looks back to see how they fit
And laughs so hard he is starting to spit.
Olli now has a star-studded head,
That looks like a bathing cap instead.

"Hang on everyone, Olli cling to my flaps,
Use all your arms, don't leave any gaps."

Here they go, shouting "Hurray!
We are having a super outstanding day."

Raymie glides slowly just above the sand
But they all think that is rather bland.
"Speed up now Raymie, we want to go fast.
After all we want a real blast."

So the stingray swoops up and comes down like soft rain.
He checks to see if the red stars remain
On Olli's head, where they belong.
No problem, they are even starting a song.

Sea folks have not seen anything like this
But agree that doing it is totally bliss.
When the ride has ended all applaud wildly,
Raymie just bows and then says mildly,
"It was my pleasure to serve you today,
But now it is time for me to say
Good bye, dear sea folks far and wide,
If you want to have fun, just ask for a ride."

As Raymie is gliding out of sight,
Six neighborly friends call it a night.

DELPHINA AND THE MIRACLE OF BIRTH

Olli and the guppies always meet at the school
But lately have not done anything real cool
Besides learning neat things from Miss Leelofay,
So today they are roaming around the bay
To find some excitement and new escapades,
To quench their yearning before it fades.

"Let's stick our heads above water and see
What kind of wonders there may be."

They do so and while they are looking about
They notice nearby a terrific spout.
"Did you see that?" One guppy points out,
"I wonder what that is all about."

"Let's move and see if we can find the spot
Where it appeared - unless you'd rather not?"

"Are you kidding, Olli, we came to the bay
For some excitement and here we'll stay."

While they argue, not looking about,
Right then appears another huge spout.
So close are the friends that it stuns them now.
What is doing that, and how?
Heads under water they're starting to shriek,
When something is touching them with a soft "beak."

"Did I scare you, that's not what I wanted to do,
Just taking a breath while coming through.
I'm a mammal, you see, and I need air,
Then spit out water with a great flair.
It is intended to keep me going,
Otherwise I would be overflowing.
I need to spew out the water collected,
Nature has that part completely perfected.
I'm a bottle nose dolphin, Delphina by name,
I'm glad that today to the bay I came.
I'm expecting my baby to be born fairly soon,
Maybe it happens today before noon."

Olli introduces himself and his group,
Delphina's delighted, turning a loop.

"That spouting you do, it looks so thrilling,
I wonder if now you would be willing
With the next spout send us above sea
And spill us all over, how would that be?"

"I would be delighted to give it a go
And it may excite baby, hopefully so
To be born to meet all of you.
That is my thought, that's what we'll do."

Olli now gathers the friends in his arms,
Moves up to the blowhole there are no "alarms."
They feel a slight rumble, Delphina lets go,
Up they all pop with a great blow.
Olli's arms open, he releases them fast
That spills them all over with a huge blast.

"Once again," says Delphina, "that will do it for me,
I am ready for baby then, as you will see."

Again they "blow up" with shouts of great fun
And when they come down, the birth has begun.
The little group stares in wonder and awe
At Delphina and the calf they never saw.
It looks just like her, but smaller, of course
And turns to the mother for its food source.
Right on her belly she has nipples he smells
And drinks 'til he's full while his mother yells:
"That's Dolphy, the baby boy I've been waiting for,
You just witnessed a miracle on the ocean floor.
Since I am a mammal, no eggs I do lay,
We have live babies as you've seen today.
Do tell your teacher what you just saw,
I am sure she also will be in great awe."

"Delphina, you blessed us with the miracle of birth,
There is no greater treasure than babies on earth.
We thank you kindly for providing much fun,
Now enjoy little Dolphy, whose life's just begun."

On the way home they are rather subdued,
Reliving the day, each in his own mood.

DORADO

Olli hums a song he just learned at school,
When he hears a voice that sounds rather cool.
Someone with the same idea uses words instead
Olli now is curious and so he turns his head:
"Hello happy singer, I'd like to meet you, please.
Would you venture closer so I can see with ease?"
Nothing happens, so he goes, following that tune
And spots the singer straight ahead fairly soon.

My goodness, he thinks, what an eerie scene,
Something so strange I have never seen.
A fish, all golden, shimmering in the sun,
His head looks smashed in, not to make fun.

He approaches him carefully, for he looks vicious
He might just eat me and think I'm delicious.
He knows how to sing and does rather well,
But what are the words? I surely can't tell.

"Good morning, strange fish, dressed up in gold,
Of your existence I've never been told.
Would you be kind and tell me your name?
I, in reply, will do the same."
The glistening fish stops, looking confused,
Yet Olli, at this point, is not amused.

"Why don't you answer when I talk to you?
Is something wrong? I could help you, too"

It is dawning on him why no answer he hears,
The words we are speaking are different, he fears.
"I am Olli" he says, pointing to his chest,
I'll just use sign language. That may be best.

The stranger looks pleased and does the same,
Touching his chest and saying his name.
"Dorado" is all our friend can make out
He's getting frustrated and starting to pout.

"Dorado", he says, "Is that your name?"
"Si," is the answer without any shame.
Admitting his failure to get anywhere,
He still wants to meet him because he does care.

"I'll just take you to Miss Leelofay,
She is learned and wise and has her way
Of communicating with many creatures,
She also will know about your features."

Olli motions the stranger to follow him
Assuring that it is just a short swim.
Dorado trusts him for he is curious too,
What the octopus has in mind and what they will do.

In the school yard they find Miss Leelofay,
She is teaching the upper classes that day.
It is recess. All students are hanging out.
They'd sure like to know what this is about.
She talks to Dorado, she understands well,
The students are anxious, as one can tell.

When she finally speaks to them with a smile
She informs them that it has been awhile
Since Dorado left Mexico, where he was born,
And once on the way he felt forlorn.
To spike up his courage to go ahead
He started to sing and that finally lead
Straight onto Olli's pathway today.
I am so glad it happened that way.
We know Olli likes to make new friends,
He is honest about it and never pretends.

"I invited Dorado to stay awhile,
To get to know him in proper style.
He'll get to know and like us, I'm sure,
The language barrier we'll have to endure."

Olli gets edgy and now wants to know
What's with his color, why does he shine so?
Why does his head look so smashed in?
Why does he have such a long dorsal fin?

Miss Leelofay explains that he was born that way
And for the rest of his life that's how he will stay.
Dorado means 'Golden' and that is his skin,
There are others like him, in many colors and fin.

The introduction has ended and life runs its way,
Dorado stays over and soon they all say
That he's not just golden, he also is smart
And learns the new language right from the start.
Olli and friends are doing the same,
They love it and look at it as a game.
The teacher is proud that it worked out well.
They all will be friends, for how long, who can tell?

THE RESCUE

Olli's day is starting out fairly rough today.
The sea is quite choppy, moving every which way.
The waves are higher than he's seen them before,
He wonders what it looks like on the shore.
He propels to the surface to find out,
What the damage of wind and waves is about.

He barely has reached the edge of the lagoon
When he hears a faint cry and notices soon
A tiny creature is struggling on the surface,
Clinging to something with great purpose.
Olli sticks out his head to listen for the sound.
Searching the surroundings 'til he finally found
The muffled voice coming from a small raft,
Bobbing along like a damaged sea craft.

Looking more like a leaf from a tree,
The kind to be found at the shore he can see.
What's on that flimsy floating device
Makes Olli now look once, then twice.
Whatever it is that is gasping for air
He never saw, but with no time to spare
He brings up one arm under the bobbing flotation,
The small creature's hoping for its salvation.

Olli lifts up the fallen leaf from the sea
And brings it closer so he can see.
The miniature creature now takes a deep breath
Glad to be rescued from certain death.
It was he who kept it from drowning today
And she wants to thank him in a big way.

"Who and what are you, kind stranger, do say,
I never have been here before today.
I heard that the nectar around here tastes great,
But I certainly did not expect this fate.
While I was happily buzzing around
Up came a wind right from the ground.
A gust took my leaf that was rather loose
And tossed me about like a drunken goose.
It blew me over the edge of the sea,
Where today, of all days, no creature should be."

"You're safe with me and will come to no harm,
As long as I keep you on my arm.
From all you have told me I still do not know
Who you are, little one that is frightened so?

I am an octopus, Olli by name,
I'm so glad that to the surface I came.
Whatever kind of creature you may be,
You certainly don't belong on the open sea."

"The water is cold and got me all wet,
It's just the element you love, I'll bet.
I am Suzee, a young free-spirited bee,
I don't follow orders well, as you can see.

I should find nectar to bring back to my hive,
But I want adventures to feel more alive.
Some day, when my roaming days are over
I'll return to the hive to make honey from clover
Which I see beyond the beach right now,
And would like to return to again, but how?"

"That should be no problem; I can help you with that
I'll toss you right over, in no time flat.
You will quickly go back to where you belong
And have sweet nectar to again get strong."

"Next time when I am near this lagoon
I'll float clover blossoms on the water at noon.
Hopefully that day you will be nearby,
To stick out your head again and say 'Hi.'
I am ready now for my toss, go ahead,
I'm tired and will go straight to bed.
Wee, buzz, buzz, buzz, I made it, good night."

SOS – SAVE OUR SEAS

After summer vacation Olli and the guppies return to school.
They are first graders now and know that learning is still cool.
Miss Leelofay has new projects to work on all year.
One disturbs her greatly and causes some fear.

"How can we save the oceans? They are home to all sea life.
Have you seen the garbage in it? It will cause much strife.
I need your help with a plan but also follow through!
Do you, my eager students, know what I'm telling you?"

"Yes, Miss Leelofay, we get it. We see trash humans leave behind
When they frolic at the sea side, how can they be so unkind?
The constant flow of the water brings what they don't take along
Right into our home, the ocean, we all think that is wrong.
Is there something we can do to make the situation right?
We are just a few sea creatures and that would be a big, big fight.
Could we really make a difference when humans do not seem to care?
Where do we start? What should be done? How can we help this sad affair?"

"Maybe we could go ashore and gather up the litter.
I've seen some humans do just that, with those we can't be bitter.
We then drop it on the beach for them to find it there
With a note to draw attention to this planet we all share.
No matter where we live, our lives and homes should be respected.
All the pollution in the water makes us feel rejected.
Let's make sea creatures aware of dangers lurking straight ahead
When they encounter rubbish, fairly soon they could be dead."

"Are you with me?" asks the teacher, "let's set a date to start our plan.
We'll knot a net of sea plants; at least we'll do the best we can.
Up and down the shore we'll swim and gather trash we find,
Checking every plant and coral, nothing will be left behind."

The class is eager to get started to knot a net and head for shore
To rid the waste from that blue water, right down to the ocean floor.
While they're out there with the teacher they soon find a horrid sight,
A turtle wrapped in plastic, struggling, choking, what a plight!

"This poor creature needs our help; let's see what I can find
To free it from the tangles, sharp coral comes to mind."

Olli finds what he is seeking and starts to cut with all his might
To remove the choke from turtle, who has given up the fight.
The grateful creature takes a breath relieved to now be free,
"I know trapped animals close by, they're suffering just like me.
They will need your help, before it is too late.
Could you find it in your heart to save them from that fate?"

With no time to waste they hurry to the mentioned spot
What they're seeing stuns them, they can believe it not.
A group of fish all tangled in a net with no escape,
The rescuers work fast and hard to free them from that "drape."

"I wish the human mess-folk's could see what they have caused,"
One of the guppies says with tears, "Perhaps they would have paused
To take along their trash and thus prevent more scenes like these.
Could someone tell them this is wrong? Could someone tell them, PLEASE?"

"Let's do what we came out for which you all understand,
Remove unwanted items now and make the sea look grand."
Miss Leelofay is eager to close the task today.
Her students all agree with her and now they're on their way.

A net full of the refuse is collected in short while,
All work hard to move that enormous garbage pile
Onto the beach for humans to find and grow aware
Of their unkind behavior, when they leave their trash out there.

Olli is chosen to create a note to go with the mound,
On a large sea leaf he writes with ink that in his body he's found:
"Please, humans, keep the oceans clean, our lives depend on you.
Its home to many creatures, and it's the right thing to do.
Thank you for considering a beach that's clean and pure.
Miss Leelofay, Olli and the guppies call that a simple cure
For mutual respect of this planet we all share,
We write for all sea creatures, because we all do care.
Respectfully submitted by sea folks everywhere.
THANK YOU SO MUCH."

CPSIA information can be obtained
at www.ICGtesting.com
Printed in the USA
BVHW021023020919
557352BV00020B/775/P